Ben's
Lucky Hat

Ben's Lucky Hat

HANS-ERIC HELLBERG

Translated from the Swedish
by Patricia Crampton

CROWN PUBLISHERS, INC.
New York

First American edition 1982 by Crown Publishers, Inc.
Copyright © 1965 by Hans-Eric Hellberg
English translation copyright © 1980 by Patricia Crampton
All rights reserved. No part of this publication may be reproduced,
stored in a retrieval system, or transmitted, in any form or by any means,
electronic, mechanical, photocopying, recording, or otherwise, without
prior written permission of the publisher. Inquiries should be addressed
to Crown Publishers, Inc., One Park Avenue, New York, New York 10016.
Originally published in Swedish as *Björn med Trollhatten*
by Albert Bonniers Förlag, Stockholm
First published in Great Britain 1980 by Methuen Children's Books Ltd.
Manufactured in the United States of America

10 9 8 7 6 5 4 3 2 1

The text of this book is set in 14 point Garamond.

Library of Congress Cataloging in Publication Data
Hellberg, Hans-Eric, 1927–
Ben's lucky hat.
Translation of: Björn med trollhatten.
Summary: When Ben becomes owner of a
funny, too-big hat, some of the more fearsome
things in his life become less so.
[1. Hats—Fiction] I. Title.
PZ7.H37417Be 1982   [Fic]   82-13038
ISBN 0-517-54825-9

Ben's
Lucky Hat

That morning it was Sammy who rang first. Ben stretched out an arm sleepily and tugged twice on the cord hanging in front of the window.

Now Sammy would know that he was awake.

On the wall opposite the window there was a Christmas bell hanging on a hook. From the bell a cord ran through the window ventilator down to the window in the apartment below and in through their ventilator. That was where Sammy's room was.

The sky was blue and clear, looking as if it had been painted. In that case, who had painted it— God?

He himself was God. Ben decided: Now I'm going to paint a motorcyclist riding along a road and the sky will be just as blue in my picture as in God's picture.

Ben jumped out of bed, got out his paints and brought water from the bathroom.

The apartment was quiet. Mom and Dad were asleep. Only the clock was ticking in the hall.

First he drew the motorcyclist. Then he filled in the helmet with yellow paint and the clothes with blue paint and the boots with brown. He painted the sky sky-blue.

He took off his glasses and looked out of the window to match the paint to the sky. If you were farsighted, as he was, you saw better at a distance without glasses. And what could be at a greater distance than the sky?

So you wouldn't need glasses if you were looking at God.

Not that he was particularly concerned with God.

It was difficult to get the paper to look like the sky. He had to admit that God was better at painting than he was. At least at painting skies. He was probably worse at riding motorcycles.

The silence around him changed, taking on more and more sounds. There was a rushing in the pipes. A car started up in the parking lot. A baby cried. Mom went into the bathroom. Dad said something. Now there were so many sounds that the silence was swallowed up. Night was over. A new day was on its way.

He was always forgetting to clean his glasses. He used his sheet. Without his glasses the colors swam together on the paper in front of him. It looked very nice. It looked like a crazy painting in one of those art books Dad had. Almost none of the pictures in the book represented anything. There were just colors and lines.

Saturday. A beautiful morning. Not the usual rush.

Mom was making noises in the kitchen today.

Dad was still in bed with the newspaper Mom had given him. Tomorrow it would be Dad who fixed breakfast and Mom who stayed in bed. She always read a lighthearted article first. Sometimes she laughed aloud. Ben liked listening to her laughter.

Dad began with the comic strip. Then he read about politics. It was all about war and how much pay people should get and who was going to become president somewhere.

Ben thought of something: What if Sammy's dad was lying in bed reading and his mother was making breakfast in the kitchen while Sammy was kneeling on the floor painting a motorcyclist riding along under a blue sky . . . ?

❦ 2

Their apartments were identical, except that they had different furniture, of course.

There were seven apartments in the building. What if there were seven dads lying in bed just now reading page 10 and seven boys on the floor painting seven skies with blue paint . . . ?

What if seven thousand mothers in the town were standing in the kitchen just now, making breakfast, and they were all called Wendy and all the fathers were called Keith and all the boys were called Ben and wore glasses?

Ben had to go to the bathroom.

What if seven hundred thousand boys wearing glasses were standing peeing in the toilet and thinking the same thought: that seven hundred thousand boys wearing glasses might be standing peeing and thinking the same thought . . . ?

"Wash your hands too!" Mom called. "Breakfast will be ready by then."

And what if all the mothers were calling to all the children . . . ?

Ben washed his hands and went to the kitchen. His head was giddy. Sometimes peculiar thoughts popped up that were hard to understand.

How many fathers were there in the whole world? A million? Several million? What if all the fathers stayed in bed . . . ?

His mother poured hot chocolate and coffee.

"Go in to Dad and tell him if he wants his oatmeal warm he had better get himself out of bed fast."

Dad was lying in bed feeling good. His cheeks looked dirty because he hadn't shaved.

"Your wife says that you'll be in trouble if you don't hurry up," said Ben.

"I want breakfast in bed."

"This isn't a hotel."

They never got tired of this game. Tomorrow it would be Mom's turn.

Dad put on his robe and went out to the kitchen.

He was a mailman, and he ran the entire post office as well.

Mom was a B.A. He didn't know what B.A. meant, but she taught at the high school.

"Are we going out to Chub Lake today?" she asked.

They had their summer cabin on Chub Lake. They could fish there, but they never caught chub. Dad insisted that there had been no chub in Chub Lake for a hundred years.

"Sammy must come too!" said Ben.

"In that case he must ask his mother first."

It was Sammy's mother who made decisions in his family. She was small and irritable and talked in a shrill voice.

"Are you going to spend the night?" she asked when Ben arrived with the invitation.

Ben nodded.

"Then you'll have to be responsible for him."

Ben nodded again.

When he was alone with Sammy he said, "Remember, I'm responsible for you now."

"Oh, go and jump in the lake," said Sammy.

❦ 3

They sat together on the back seat. Mom drove fast along the winding gravel road to Chub Lake.

Sammy didn't keep still for a second. He was always getting excited when something unusual was going on. He had pajamas and boots and a toothbrush and a sweat shirt, in case it got cold, in a plastic bag. It was warm in the car. The sun was hot.

"Do you think we can fish?" asked Sammy. "And swim perhaps? Do you remember that pike I got on my line?"

Sammy was tall and fair. His eyebrows were almost white and he had masses of freckles on his nose.

Ben never thought about how Sammy looked. Sammy was just Sammy.

Ben put his hand in his pocket. That was where he kept Woody. He smoothed Woody's polished surface with his thumb and forefinger.

Woody was a scrap of wood that he had gotten

from his grandfather, who was a carpenter. He was a foreman in a furniture factory. In the corners of the factory there was always a thick layer of sawdust and wood shavings. If you searched through it you could find the most fantastic things that had been left over: wonderful lathe-turned bed legs, little wheels, cubes, rings, all made of wood. They smelled good and were nice to hold in your hand.

Woody was a turned fragment of wood, smooth as porcelain but softer, with two knotholes that looked like eyes and a mark he had made into a mouth. Woody was his secret thing. Only Sammy knew about it and knew what it meant. But he did not know quite how *much* Woody meant to Ben.

Ben never went out without Woody. He never started on anything without touching Woody first.

Woody brought him luck.

🌳 4

The summer cabin was painted red. A narrow path wound down to the beach between stones and tree roots. There was an old iron pot there that Mom used to boil dirty clothes in during the summer.

The rowboat was pulled up on the beach. You only had to push it out into the water and row across the lake.

The first thing Dad did when he arrived was to work. The first thing Mom did was to work. And they were on vacation!

They prepared food and carried up water in buckets and moved stones and nailed fence railings and painted window frames and made a food pantry and repaired the roof. . . . It never ended.

When you were on vacation you were supposed to play. You were supposed to relax and only do things that were fun and forget about all the boring things.

That day Ben suddenly understood. Working

on the summer cabin was their way of having fun, of playing. When he looked more closely at them he could see that they were different, more relaxed, easier, and happier. They sometimes smiled at each other without saying a word.

They had changed their clothes. Dad was wearing overalls and boots and had a crumpled hat on his head. Mom had on light blue jeans, a cherry-red shirt and signal-yellow boots. She kept her hair in place with a blue headband.

Imagine her going to school looking like that! And as happy as that! The other teachers would be absolutely flabbergasted.

Ben giggled.

"What is it?" asked Sammy.

"Flabbergasted," said Ben. "It's a nice word. Do you know what flabbergasted is?"

"Fried fish?"

"No. A teacher in Mom's school. That's what he looks like."

What did a flabbergast look like? When you were flabbergasted you threw your hands up in surprise.

Doctor Flabbergast was ten feet tall, with a head no bigger than an orange. When he talked, music came out of his mouth instead of words. His students never learned anything in his class, but they liked the music.

10

Sometimes they danced to the music when he was telling a long story about Napoleon or Churchill.

"What are you grinning about?"

Ben could not talk about his crazy ideas. There were some things you had to keep to yourself, even from your best friend.

❦ 5

They did all the things they wanted to do. Sammy caught three little catfish. Ben got tangled up in his line and scratched his cheek on the hook, just under the eye. Mom cleaned the scratch with something that burned like fire. Then she put a Band-Aid on it. It felt good and tough.

It was hot in the sun but too cold to swim, so they waded. But they kept near the shore, between the jetty and the boat.

Ben wanted Mom to make a fire under the pot and fill it with water. Then they could bathe in the pot and pretend they were being cooked by cannibals.

"Nonsense!" said Mom.

Grown-ups said "nonsense" about lots of things that were fun.

Perhaps that was the reason why they so seldom had fun themselves. There were plenty of grouchy, nagging grown-ups. They ought to go in for some nonsense and not always be so uptight.

12

When they had waded until they were shivering they lay on their backs on the jetty looking up at the clouds. Ben liked to feel the warm wood under his fingers, like lying on a huge Woody!

Mom and Dad fixed up a picnic on a hill with a view of the lake. Mom got a sap stain from the pine trees on her best slacks. It was impossible to get out. The sap smelled wonderful.

Then Dad almost fell off the roof.

Full from the picnic the boys disappeared into the woods in search of adventure. They got lost in ten minutes. Then they wandered around before they discovered that they had ended up on the other side of the lake. They could see the cabin from where they were.

Ben held on tightly to Woody in his pocket. It was Woody who had seen them through.

They followed the beach back again and Ben stumbled over a tree root here and there.

When they got home they were thirsty and tired and happy. But Mom and Dad had not even missed them!

✿ 6

The most exciting thing was spending the night in the cabin. They were allowed to sleep by themselves in bunk beds in the attic. Ben let Sammy have the top bunk.

As there was no light they had to undress in the dark. A little light came up from the kitchen, where a gas lamp hung from the ceiling.

Ben took off his glasses. Sammy looked fuzzy, like a shadow.

When Ben was putting on his pajamas he stumbled against Sammy and pulled him down with him.

"What's the matter with you?"

"I tripped," said Ben.

"Well, watch it!"

Sammy started to play at wrestling and got Ben on his back with an arm grip. The back of Ben's head hit the floor.

"Are you beaten?"

"Yes."

14

They got up. Ben could not find his pajama leg with his foot. He stumbled again.

Suddenly it was fun to fall down. They tripped each other, punched each other, bumped into stools and hit the walls.

"I see so badly without glasses," squeaked Sammy.

"I'm blind," said Ben in a deep voice.

He put out his arms and went straight for Sammy. They tumbled in a heap, giggling.

Dad's voice: "Are you ever going to be quiet up there?"

Giggle. Giggle.

"I'll come up, then!"

No more giggles.

They lay still and silent on the floor, side by side. Then Sammy clambered up into his bunk and Ben crawled down under the quilt. It smelled of old wood and moss and paraffin and tobacco smoke.

Ben stared up in the darkness. Sammy was right over his head. They didn't need to ring any bells now. They just had to stretch out a hand and give the other a shake.

"What is it?"

"You'd better not wet the bed tonight."

Sammy giggled.

Ben grinned to himself. Soon he was asleep.

Something woke him up—a strange sound.

At first he did not know where he was. The room was pitch dark. Above his head was a darker shadow, as if the ceiling had dropped in the night or as if he were sleeping in a chest with the lid closed. . . .

A tapping sound, as if thousands of little animals were trotting around on the roof just above him. It was raining.

And the rain was so close because they were staying in the summer cabin by Chub Lake. Sammy was with him. He was even closer than the rain, but he didn't know that. He was asleep.

Mom and Dad were sleeping in the room next to the kitchen. Outside in the woods the birds and squirrels and badgers and moose were sleeping too.

Did moose sleep standing up? He had seen a picture of a moose leaning against a tree trunk, fast asleep.

Perhaps the squirrels had been awakened by the

rain, just like him, and were listening to the rustling and rattling of the raindrops among the leaves and pine needles.

One thing was certain: Squirrels did not sleep standing up. They crept into their dry hole and curled up with their tails spread over them up to the chin and snoozed in warmth and safety until the birds woke them up. The sun woke the birds.

The sun never slept.

✿ 8

The next time, Ben was awakened by a delicious smell. He opened his eyes. Sammy was standing beside the bed, holding a slice of gingerbread under his nose.

Ben snatched the gingerbread and sank his teeth into it.

"Have you been awake long?"

"All morning," said Sammy.

There were clashing sounds from the kitchen. Ben was certain that it was Dad who was making breakfast. Mom was lying in bed reading or dozing, just as it should be.

It was still raining.

The boys got dressed. Ben could see out over the lake through the little north window. The day was dull gray and misty, the outlines were blurred. It looked cold. The jetty was frosty and the boat was half full of water.

They sat near the stove, eating breakfast. The wood in the stove crackled.

"Shall we go home?" asked Dad.

"It doesn't look as though it's going to clear," Mom said.

There was a fresh smell of pine and moss when they went out. The boys ran down to the jetty, skidding on wet tree roots in their boots. The boat smelled of fish.

They dipped their fingers in the water. It was lukewarm.

"Perhaps we could swim," said Sammy doubtfully.

"Or fish," said Ben. "They bite well in rainy weather."

"We're going now!" Mom called.

✤ 9

The next day Ben's uncle and aunt came on a surprise visit just in time for lunch. Mom smiled and Dad growled; Ben could see that their guests were not welcome.

Dad had not even bothered to shave. They had thought of having sandwiches and hot chocolate. . . .

Now they would have to think of something more elegant. Dad was mad.

Ben's aunt did not notice anything. She talked all the time and did not help with the work. She was that kind of aunt.

Ben didn't like her voice. It was much too shrill. She reminded him of Sammy's mother. As soon as he could, Ben went to his room.

On the wall was a hard clay mask, showing the face of a man with a long chin and scarred cheeks. His uncle had brought it from Africa a year ago.

On the desk stood a china dog called Max.

Above the bed hung a picture of seven gnomes dancing in a meadow.

Ben cleaned his glasses and put them on again. It had stopped raining.

The bell on the wall opposite his window rang.

Ben opened the window and looked down.

Sammy was looking up from the window below.

"I've thought of a way we can earn some money."

"What is it?"

"I've been reading in the paper about a man who pays twenty cents apiece for frogs."

"For frogs? What does he want them for?"

"I don't know. But I know where we can catch as many as we like. In Little Lake. Coming?"

"I don't know. . . ."

"What are you doing?"

"Nothing special."

"I've got a fishing net. All you need is a plastic bucket. We might catch hundreds!"

"Okay, I'll come."

He hurried to the door, turned back and pulled out one of the drawers in his desk. There was a cap pistol in it. He made sure it was loaded and put it in his pocket. Then he took the red plastic bucket from the kitchen.

Sammy was waiting for him. He got into the elevator with a blue plastic bucket and a butterfly net.

They kicked the wall of the elevator as they rode down. Sammy made faces at his reflection in the glass.

When they came out onto the steps Ben took Woody out of his pocket, looked at him, squeezed him hard and put him back in his pocket. Sammy nodded. This was an old ritual.

Woody belonged to Ben, but there was some of his power and magic to spare for Sammy as well. That was why he had nodded.

Kevin and Ian and a few others were playing soccer in the garden. Kevin shouted:

"Sammy! Would you like to be the goalie?"

"Might as well."

"Come on then."

"What about Ben?"

"We don't need any more."

"Then I'm not coming either."

"Ben's clumsy. He trips all the time."

"Ben can't help not seeing very well."

"But he's afraid of the ball."

"Do you want a goalie or not?"

Kevin shrugged his shoulders. Ben and Sammy left their bikes and joined in the game. Sammy was a good goalie: fearless, lively and fast.

Ben was bad at ball games: Because of his far-sightedness, the nearer the ball came, the more out of focus it seemed, and so he often missed it. He was uncertain and slow and tripped over his own feet in his eagerness to play well.

He would have preferred to play alone with Sammy, but Sammy liked team games.

They kicked the ball around for a bit. Ben was playing back. He accidentally kicked the ball into his own goal. Sammy threw himself on the ball but he couldn't prevent the goal. Sammy hissed:

"What good was that? Clumsy!"

Ben hung his head.

At last Sammy got tired of playing and they bicycled out of town. Ben had a blue bicycle and a red bucket. Sammy had a red bicycle and a blue bucket.

In the distance they could hear church bells ringing. They cycled across flat country. There was a little wind.

Sammy rode ahead, annoyed with Ben for giving the other team a goal.

Ben rode behind him, waiting patiently for Sammy to forgive him.

When they rode past the cemetery they saw a funeral procession on its way to an open grave. Curious, they put their bikes down and approached cautiously.

"What's that?" asked Ben.

"A burial. Haven't you ever seen a burial before?"

"No. Have you?"

"No."

"Why are they going so slowly?"

"There's no hurry now. After all, he's dead."

"Who?"

"Whoever is in the coffin."

The procession reached the open grave. The coffin was lowered into the hole.

The boys went as close as they could.

The priest picked up a little trowel and sprinkled earth on the coffin.

"From earth you came, to earth you shall return. . . ."

The mourners laid flowers on the coffin lid. One or two people made short speeches. Others simply bowed their heads.

"Why do they do that?"

"They're saying good-bye for the last time."

The mourners moved quietly away. One woman was crying into her handkerchief.

The boys went hesitantly toward the grave. They looked down at the flower-heaped box. Sammy copied the priest and threw in a handful of earth:

24

"From earth you came, and in the earth you shall lie. . . ."

They played at being mourners and bowed their heads.

"Would you like to see our grave?" asked Sammy. "Grandmother is buried here."

They looked at Sammy's grandmother's grave. It was nicely kept, with raked sand and flowers growing in a semicircle in front of the gravestone. Sammy took a little fork and filled in the raked furrows. He rearranged the flowers.

"Grandmother will be pleased now."

"But she won't see it."

"Well, that's what they say."

✣ 10

They bicycled along a gravel track on the edge of an airfield.

A glider rose into the air above the treetops just ahead of them. They put on their brakes.

The glider was going to land. They could clearly see the pilot sitting under his plexiglass hood. He was wearing dark glasses and his right hand lay lightly on the control stick. The flaps were out on the wings. They could hear a whining sound.

The glider approached the ground rapidly, glided over the grass at a height of a few yards and descended gently. It landed on one wheel, the tail went down and the glider rolled on for fifty or sixty yards. When it stopped the left wing tipped toward the ground.

"I would like to fly like that!" exclaimed Ben.

"You can't have anything wrong with your eyes if you're going to be a pilot," said Sammy.

"How do you know?" asked Ben.

"I've heard it."

"But I can see very well at a distance. That must be the main thing if you're going to fly."

Sammy shook his head.

They left their bikes in a ditch and threw themselves down in the grass. A propeller-driven plane started up, with a glider behind it on a towline. A man in overalls with big pockets on the legs ran alongside, holding up the left wing. Soon the plane and glider were traveling so fast that he had to let go.

Ben sighed. He had become so involved in watching the flight that he hadn't moved a muscle. His mouth was half open. He took off his glasses and followed the planes. They were heading for some high clouds.

He wished he were with them; that it was he who was sitting in the silent glider with the joystick between his knees, cushioned by the air and wheeling about like a bird.

His eyes *would* be good enough!

That lucky man, sitting up there among the clouds, in loneliness and silence, close to heaven. . . .

Then the pilot released the towrope. The plane dived, with the towline hanging free behind it. Just over the airfield the pilot released the line, which came whistling down from the sky.

"Let's go," said Sammy.

27

"Not yet."

"There's nothing going on here."

What was he waiting for? For the plane to do loops and rolls, for it to crash onto the field?

"Now the glider is right under that cloud that looks like a begging dog."

"I can't see anything," said Sammy.

Ben could see it clearly. The glider was rising. It circled around and around.

"I don't want to be a real pilot," said Ben. "Not the kind that flies passenger planes. Just one like that, without an engine. It wouldn't matter so much about my eyes then, would it?"

"I don't know," said Sammy. "Are we going to collect frogs or not?"

Ben wanted to watch the glider landing but it seemed to take a long time. It was growing smaller and smaller.

"Let's go."

⚘ 11

There was a sign in front of them. Written on it in large letters was:

MILITARY TRAINING AREA

NO ADMISSION

Sammy cycled on, not taking any notice.

"Stop!" called Ben. "We're not allowed to ride through here!"

"Oh, I've been here lots of times. It doesn't matter."

"Didn't you see the sign?"

"Of course I did. Are you scared?"

Who was scared of a sign? And who was scared when he was with Sammy? Ben rode after his friend.

Little Lake was not much bigger than a pond, overgrown with water lilies, bulrushes, and marsh marigolds. The water was greenish black and still as oil, full of little creatures on and under the surface.

There were not as many frogs as Sammy had

said. There was actually a shortage of frogs and they were difficult to catch.

Ben held on to the plastic buckets while Sammy swung the butterfly net.

It took an hour to catch two frogs. By that time they were tired and sick of it all.

Ben took out his cap pistol.

"Hands up!"

"I'm not scared of you."

Sammy jumped behind a tree. Ben fired and missed. Sammy took out his own pistol, poked it out from behind the tree and fired.

But Ben was already lying safely behind a boulder. He wriggled cautiously to one side and scrambled down into a cleft. Then he ran to the other side, climbed up and crept forward. Now he was behind Sammy.

"Drop your gun or I fire!"

Sammy spun around. Then Ben fired.

"You're dead!"

"Not at all," said Sammy. "You only wounded me. You hit me in the shoulder."

"I hit you in the heart."

"You hit me in the shoulder! I've seen them on TV and they always hit the shoulder! And you don't die of that. You just hunch around with one bad arm."

Sammy dangled his arm at his side. Ben laughed.

Suddenly the silence exploded in a cross fire of machine guns.

Ben and Sammy flung themselves to the ground. Holding on to each other, they tried to hide behind a tangle of roots.

"They're firing!" said Ben. "It's war!"

"It's not war," said Sammy. "It's just practice."

"But they're firing! It said on the sign that we couldn't come in. What if they hit us!"

They clung together. Two soldiers moved stealthily forward, machine guns ready. They almost stumbled over the boys.

"What are you doing here?" one of the soldiers asked.

"Playing," said Sammy.

"You're in a military training area. You're not allowed here."

"Why not?"

"We're practicing for war here."

"We're playing war, too."

"We're not playing!"

"Is it for real?" said Ben.

"Yes. Look."

The soldier raised his weapon slowly until it was pointing at his companion's stomach. He waited for three seconds. Then he let off a short burst of automatic fire.

The soldier doubled up, staggered a few steps, swayed to and fro, uttered a gurgling sound, sank to his knees, collapsed and died in typical movie style.

Ben and Sammy were shocked. For a few seconds they were convinced that it was real.

Then the dead soldier began to laugh. He jumped up and mowed down his companion and the boys. They died in contorted positions of make-believe death.

A little way off, the rest of the platoon was playing the same game. Machine guns chattered in close combat among the trees.

Suddenly all the weapons were silent. Someone pretended to moan. Someone else laughed.

And then they heard the sound of the church bells sweeping across the plain. Another funeral.

Ben and Sammy bicycled home.

⚘ 12

That evening they played in Ben's room. Later Ben could not remember what they had done. Painted? Played with cars? Played a game?

Sammy's mother called and told him to come home early. Before leaving, he asked as always:

"Coming tomorrow?"

And Ben gave the usual answer.

"Why did you go so far away?" asked Dad at supper.

"We were going to catch frogs."

"What an idea!"

"You get twenty cents apiece if you send them to a laboratory."

"What laboratory?"

"I don't know. Sammy read about it in the paper."

"I read it too," said Mom. "A research laboratory is asking for frogs for experiments."

"How many did you catch?" asked Dad.

"Two, Sammy has them."

"How are you going to send them?"

"In a box with air holes."

"It's bare faced cruelty to animals!" said Dad. "Not to speak of what happens to the frogs in the laboratory."

"Frogs don't feel anything," said Ben.

"Haven't you ever heard a frog shriek when it was hurt? It's horrible."

"We would have earned ten dollars apiece if we had caught a hundred frogs."

"What would you do with all that money?"

"I don't know. Buy candy, for one thing. And a magnifying glass. And a knife, perhaps. Sammy thought of buying a bow and arrow."

"It's a good thing there weren't many frogs," said Mom.

"They were hard to catch. And then we were sent away."

"By whom?"

"Soldiers."

"You weren't in a military area, were you?"

"Yes."

"But it's forbidden, isn't it?"

"Yes. But Sammy said it didn't matter."

"Sammy is bold and careless," said Dad.

"You could have gotten into trouble," said Mom.

"No danger," said Ben. "They were firing blank cartridges."

34

"Firing?"

"Just pretend. Like when we play with our cap pistols."

"It's dangerous, in any case," said Dad. "It's no place for little boys."

"I'm not a little boy."

"Sometimes you are. You must never ride to Little Lake alone again!"

"I wasn't alone. Sammy was with me."

"You know what I mean. Without grown-ups. It's too far away. The traffic is dangerous."

"Oh, everything's dangerous!"

"We're not exactly living in paradise."

"Would you like more pudding?" asked Mom.

"I'm full," Ben said. "Are you staying home tonight?"

"Unfortunately, no. We have been invited to a party. . . ."

"You're always out in the evenings!"

"We try to be at home as much as possible, but there's so much to do."

"What about me?"

"You're big enough to look after yourself now."

"Before I was a little boy! Which way do you want it?"

Mom and Dad exchanged glances.

"One for you," said Mom.

"And you," said Dad.

✲ 13

Ben was sitting on the floor gluing matchboxes together into a pyramid when the bell rang. Dad was in the shower. He caught a glimpse of Mom through the open door. She was just putting on one of her prettiest dresses.

He opened the window and leaned out.

"I've got something for you," said Sammy. "Hoist away!"

There was another cord beside the signal cord. It had been left there since the time when Ben had measles and could not have visitors because of infection. When the bell rang he pulled up the cord and hoisted in a bag of chocolate or a book or a magazine. It was great fun. But it was a bore having measles. And it was lonely when Mom and Dad were out at the same time.

Ben hoisted up a plastic bucket. There was a frog in the bucket.

"That's yours," said Sammy.

What could he do with the frog? A frog was

not like a dog, which you could teach to do tricks.

Or could you? Ben tried to teach the frog to jump over the pyramid. It didn't want to. It was a stupid frog.

Everyone knew that frogs were good at jumping. Why didn't this frog jump? It just sat breathing with its throat and looking silly.

"Go to bed now, Ben," Mom said, looking in on him.

"I'm not tired."

"You know you have to be in bed when we go out."

Dragging his feet, he went to the bathroom and brushed his teeth. It was wet in there after Dad's and Mom's showers. The mirror had fogged up.

When he came back, the frog was gone. Maybe it had jumped over the pyramid.

He was going to keep small things in there when it was finished. You stuck a little tack with a big head through the end of each box. Then you could open the boxes by pulling the tacks. He would have foreign coins in one box, rubber bands in another, paper clips in a third, pins in a fourth, chalks in a fifth and throat lozenges in a sixth.

"Aren't you in bed yet?" Mom asked from his doorway.

He had forgotten what he was supposed to be doing.

"I'm looking for something."

"You can do that tomorrow. Into bed now!"

Mom tiptoed back into her bedroom in her stockinged feet.

Ben searched his room. No frog. He was just pushing back the covers to get into bed when he heard a shriek from his parents' bedroom. Ben ran toward it. Mom was standing on a stool, looking terrified. She had on only one shoe.

Dad came rushing in from the hall.

"What is it?"

"Take it away!" Mom yelled.

"What do you mean?"

"Mom's found my frog," said Ben.

Just then the frog jumped out of Mom's other shoe.

"Take it!" shouted Mom.

Dad began to laugh.

"If you could see yourself!"

"If you don't take that disgusting frog away I don't know what I'll do!" said Mom.

Dad shook his head. At that moment the frog took a long leap toward him. He stopped laughing and ran out the door.

"Coward!" cried Mom. "You ought to see yourself. Pathetic!"

Ben got the plastic bucket and scooped the frog into it. A little later Dad took the bucket down to the car to empty out the frog in a nearby lake when he and Mom went to the party.

At last Ben was in bed. He didn't like being left alone. The apartment suddenly became so large that he felt he had shrunk.

Crazy thoughts kept coming and he could not stop them. What if the Invisible Man came rushing in . . . ? What if he got a pain in his side and didn't know what to do . . . ? What if the doorbell rang . . . ?

Luckily he was tired. He reached for a book but couldn't read it. His eyelids were so heavy. . . .

He was allowed to have the light on until his parents came home. The seven gnomes danced on the wall above his bed. It was his favorite painting. He looked at the gnomes, shut his eyes and slept.

❧ 14

The next day was cloudy, but it didn't rain. Dad and Mom sat silently at the breakfast table, eating very little. It was like that every time after a party. They looked glum and had not had enough sleep.

Ben made a mixture of cocoa, sugar and milk. He played with the sticky mess in the cup and licked his spoon.

Dad was reading the newspaper.

The sound of an ambulance siren came nearer and nearer.

In the end the sound was piercingly high and then it suddenly stopped. Ben ran to the window.

The ambulance had stopped outside their apartment house. Two men dressed in white got out with a stretcher.

A car was standing half across the road. Buckled under its front wheel lay Sammy's red bicycle.

The men put the stretcher down on the pavement and picked up a small figure.

Ben took off his glasses to see better at that distance.

They laid Sammy on the stretcher and pushed the stretcher into the ambulance.

"It's Sammy," said Ben.

"Are you sure?" asked his mother.

"I recognize his coat and his bike. He's been run over by a car."

Dad joined him at the window and looked down.

The ambulance was driving away with the siren on and the light rotating on the roof.

"Do you think he's hurt?" asked Ben. But he knew the answer.

"It looks like it," said his mother. "I'll call the hospital soon and ask. You must get ready for school."

Ben nodded. He went to his room and collected his books. The seven gnomes were dancing on the wall.

The signal cord. He tugged it hesitantly. There was no answer.

He had known that in advance, so why had he pulled the cord?

He put his hand in his pocket and squeezed Woody.

Teeth. Mom always asked him if he had brushed his teeth. He went to the bathroom.

When he came out again his mother was standing in the hall looking strange. Ben knew something was wrong.

"When's he coming home?"

"It will be a long time. . . ."

"Has he been hurt bad?"

"Yes."

"Very bad?"

"Yes."

"I want to see him."

"Not now."

"When?"

"When he's better."

Ben knew Mom was not telling the truth.

Sammy was not sick. Sammy was dead. And when you're dead you don't suffer.

"Sammy's dead, isn't he?" said Ben.

"Yes. But you mustn't be sad. It was so quick. . . ."

"He wasn't in pain, was he?"

"No."

"I must leave for school now."

"Yes. . . ."

Ben went down in the elevator. He kicked the wall once.

In the mirror he saw a boy, alone, with a little chocolate stuck in the corner of his mouth. He licked it off.

✤ 15

The teacher talked about Sammy at school.

"You mustn't forget your friend. He's in heaven, watching you while you play and he can hear what you say."

During the break she talked to Ben.

"You mustn't be sad."

"I'm not sad," said Ben.

"Sammy was a nice boy."

"Yes."

"And good in school."

Sammy had been best at arithmetic.

"It was just that he was so careless. You must promise to be careful."

"Yes," said Ben, not understanding what the teacher meant.

"Especially with cars. It was a car that... Watch out for the traffic."

Ben had been thinking about something.

"Can Sammy hear what I'm saying?"

"In a way."

"Is Sammy dead?"

"Yes. But you mustn't be sad."

"What's it like being dead?" asked Ben.

"You go to heaven."

"Is it far to heaven?"

"Very far."

"Can I go there?"

"You'll go there one day, when you're old."

Mom and Dad said that heaven was just pretend.

Who was he to believe?

His teacher believed in heaven. She had said he would go there when he was old. But why had Sammy gone there now, when he was only a child?

And if heaven was pretend, where did you go when you died?

Into the ground.

Where was Sammy now?

One evening Ben stood at the window, looking up at the stars. It was a clear night. He whispered:

"Sammy."

It felt as if Sammy were right beside him. He could almost touch him. Sammy wasn't all that far away after all. The grown-ups didn't know.

He knew more, because Sammy was his friend. So he wasn't sad.

44

✾ 16

Every day Ben went down in the elevator alone.
Sometimes he stuck out his tongue at the boy in
the mirror.

"You're mean!"

He didn't know why he said it, but he didn't
like the boy in the mirror and the boy in the mirror did not like him. As soon as he stuck his
tongue out the boy in the mirror put his tongue
out.

He kicked the wall.

"Sammy."

He said the name softly.

Had the boy in the mirror noticed him saying
"Sammy"?

Ben turned around quickly.

No, the boy in the mirror knew nothing. Good.
The name Sammy had become a dangerous secret.

The elevator stopped. Ben stepped out into the
hall. Before going out the door he put his hand in
his pocket and drew out Woody.

"Here . . ."

As usual he stopped on the steps for a minute to let his eyes get used to the outside.

The stone he was leaning against was warmed by the sun, which had been shining all day. It was the end of September now and the maples in the park on the way to school looked like flaming fires.

Children were playing in front of a garage. Ben called:

"Can I play too?"

Ian and Bill looked sideways at him, but they did not say anything.

Ben went nearer and repeated the question.

"Get going!" said Kevin.

Ben went to the bicycle stand and got onto a woman's bike. He pretended that the bike was a moped. He rode quickly out of the park onto the street and turned left and left again, until he was on the big road leading out of town. The engine stuttered. He turned the wheel and rode as fast as possible. He was riding away from everyone.

He was going to ride to Sammy.

He didn't know the way, but if he rode as fast as he could for a long, long time he thought he would reach Sammy in the end.

The children were shouting. He could hear the sound of the bat when they hit the ball. He did not have to strain to see. You could hear from the sound when Kevin was batting. When Kevin was batting, the fielders had to stand a long way back. He was strong. Once he had hit the ball right out into the road. It had hit a car and damaged the paint and Kevin's dad had had to pay for it.

He knew Kevin did not like to play with him because he was clumsy and couldn't see very well, but sooner or later he was usually allowed to join in.

If he waited for a while they usually called him and let him play with them.

It had been easier when Sammy was alive.

They did not call him.

⚘ 17

Ben stopped the bike and turned his head. He looked up to the kitchen window on the fifth floor.

There was a box in the window. He could see it clearly. It was an orange box with *Bournville Cocoa* printed on it; he could see it even from this far away. But close up, he could not read the small letters without his glasses.

Otherwise the kitchen window was empty. No sign of Mom. He watched for a long time but she did not come. As a rule she looked out regularly to see where he was.

Well, now he was sitting on a woman's bike, swinging to and fro, out of meanness. You shouldn't do that. The front wheel might get twisted so that the bike could not be ridden.

Serve them right, the grown-ups!

The door of the building opened and Mom came out. Putting the bike in the bicycle stand, Ben ducked behind the stand and crept away be-

48

hind a car. He crept around the corner of the house, ran across the grass and ducked through a hole in the hedge. He tripped over a tree root and fell.

"Shit!" he said.

He knew it was a bad word and he felt bad as he said it. Kevin said it all the time. He knew more bad words than anyone else.

Ben had grazed his hand on a sharp stone. A little blood came out, but it didn't hurt. Ben was used to falling over and hurting himself. He was an expert at taking tumbles.

Behind the hedge there was a ditch and on the other side of the ditch there was a fence. Beyond the fence was an orchard with apple trees and a lady with two cats and a man who chopped wood.

Sometimes the cats climbed over the fence and made a mess on the babies' sandpile.

Ben climbed over the fence. He was scared. He still remembered the time his shoe got stuck between the fence posts when he was trying to jump down, and he had almost broken his leg.

This was the first time he had been alone in the orchard.

One of the cats, Tiger, was sitting behind the porch steps, lying in wait for little birds. Tiger had gray stripes, like the mat Ben's mother had on the kitchen floor.

Ben walked quietly along the raspberry rows, ready to turn back if the porch door opened. The lady was no trouble, but you couldn't be sure about the man. He didn't look as if he liked children.

Nothing happened. Tiger's tail flicked but he continued to sit by the steps. The sun flooded over the currant bushes and behind him he could hear the shouts and laughter of the boys playing ball.

He reached the toolshed. There was a moldy smell of old wood mixed with the fresh scent of newly cut birch. A ladder was leaning against the toolshed roof. He thought about climbing it but he did not dare. Someone might come.

He wondered whether he should cross it. It had been much easier when Sammy was alive. One of them would ask:

"What shall we do?"

And the other would say they would climb trees or play in the sandpit or play ball.

Now he had no one to ask.

❦ 18

The orchard seemed very big as he stood there.

If he went back now he might be allowed to play ball, but he didn't want to anymore. He wanted to be alone.

He felt happier once he had decided.

Before going on he took Woody out of his pocket and ran his thumb over the smooth wood.

Then he went behind the toolshed. He squeezed through between two garbage cans and moved slowly forward through the tall grass, stamping down the nettles so that he would not get stung. Then he had to climb over another fence. It was very difficult because the planks were close together and had pointed tops. He caught one sleeve of his sweat shirt on a nail and had to tug hard before he could free it.

He found himself in a deep ditch with more tall grass and a lot of nettles. Although he was very careful he got stung twice.

On the other side of the hedge was a small park

with maple trees. He ran quickly over the soft grass and stopped by one of the trees. Cars were driving past outside the park.

On a park bench a little way off a man and woman were talking loudly. He listened for a few seconds.

"That's a funny hat," she said.

"What do you mean, funny?" he asked.

"A silly hat. I don't want to go out with you if you're going to wear that hat," she said.

"It's an expensive hat," he said. "From Scotland."

"I don't care about that," she said. "It's ugly and it looks awful on you."

"Okay," he said. "What do I care about an old hat? It's you I care about!"

The man took off the hat and threw it away. The hat sailed in a wide arc over the grass and fell to the ground right in front of Ben's feet.

The man got up and said:

"Shall we go?"

"Without the hat?" she said.

"I never want to see it again," he said.

When they were out of sight Ben sat down on the grass with his back against the tree and drew the hat toward him. It was speckled green and brown and it was soft. Ben liked it as soon as he felt it in his hands. It was made of coarse tweed. A faint scent of hair oil and tobacco rose from it.

Ben laughed happily to himself and put it on. It was too big, but not enough to matter.

He laughed to himself again. It was a lucky hat. It was as if he had felt happy inside as soon as the hat was on his head.

"A magic hat," he whispered.

It felt heavy on his head, like a king's crown.

He got up, feeling solemn. He was the king now and everyone had to obey him. He commanded the maple tree:

"Get me an ice cream!"

He waited a few seconds, then stretched out his hand and pretended to be holding an ice-cream cone. It was just the one he had wanted: it was soft with hard chocolate on the outside.

He pulled the hat down to his ears and ran. That felt good too.

But the hat was a little heavy. He wobbled, tripped and fell. Something bright glinted in the grass in front of him. He picked it up. It was a fifty-cent piece. A whole, shining fifty cents.

He got up and gazed at the coin on his palm, feeling weak at the knees.

It was a magic hat!

He stood where he was for a few seconds, almost

shivering. Then he knew what he had to do: He had to take off the hat. You had to be very careful with things that had magic in them.

You had to save them and use them only on special occasions.

He carefully removed the hat, holding it in both hands, and stroked it with his fingers. He felt a kind of shudder go through him. Anything might happen now!

❧ 19

Ben walked across the park, kicking the fallen leaves in front of him. The maples blazed in the sun.

To his right was the school, looking odd with its empty playground. The windows seemed to be sleeping.

He crossed the road to a candy store and walked in. He put the fifty-cent piece on the counter.

"Ice cream," he said.

"What sort do you want?"

"One with chocolate on it," said Ben.

The woman fetched an ice-cream cone and as she held it across the counter she caught sight of the hat Ben was holding in one hand.

"Do you go around in that hat?" she asked.

Ben thought it was a silly question, but he nodded his head.

"Is it your own hat?" asked the woman.

Ben realized that she was trying to make a joke.

"Yes, it is," he said.

The woman looked at him with the kind of expression grown-ups wear when they think children are lying to them.

"Little boys like you don't have hats," she said.

Little!

Just before he had been a king with a crown on his head and had found fifty cents in the grass. Ben smiled at the memory.

"Why are you laughing?" the woman asked sharply.

"I'm not laughing," he said.

"I think you're trying to make a fool of me," she said. "You had better tell me where you got that hat."

Ben could feel the tears welling up inside him. But he was not going to cry in here.

"It's my hat," he said.

The woman put out her hand.

"I don't believe that," she said. "You'd better give me the hat and I can find out who it belongs to."

Ben was panic-stricken. After all, the man who owned the hat had thrown it away. That must mean he didn't want it anymore. And it must mean that anyone who found it could keep it.

The woman snatched at the hat but Ben was too quick for her. He turned and ran. He did not look where he was going and bumped into a newspaper stand. Papers were scattered all over the floor. Terrified, he shouted:

"It wasn't my fault!"

There were tears in his eyes now and he could see less than ever. The woman was coming around the counter, probably to catch him. But she was tiptoeing carefully so as not to step on the newspapers. He fumbled at the door, found the door handle, opened the door and tumbled out.

One thing was clear: He must get away from here as fast as possible.

Everything was foggy. He blinked hard to get the tears out of his eyes and began to run along the pavement. Behind him the woman was shouting at him to stop, but he kept on running.

He ran as fast as he could for a long way, until he was so out of breath that he had to slow down. He did not dare to turn his head to see if the woman was following him.

He crossed the road into a small street and then turned into another street. As he ran he grew more and more frightened. What if the woman was following him! What if she told some other grownup to catch him!

Ben ran and ran. At last he was so tired and out of breath that he could not take one more step. He stopped and looked around. There was nobody behind him.

He was surrounded by big houses which he did not recognize. He had no idea where he was.

⚘ 20

Ben knew he had done the wrong thing. He had done something he should not have done and the magic had punished him.

Maybe he shouldn't have bought ice cream with the money the magic hat had given him. Or maybe he shouldn't have bought anything at all. But then what was the money for?

It was an impossible problem.

There was no one after him, but someone might turn up at any time. He must hide. But where?

If only he had been at home.

That was a silly thought. The woman had recognized him and knew where he lived. She might have gone to his house and told his mother what he had done and the woman might be sitting in the living room now, waiting for him.

He could not go home.

His hands felt sticky and cold. He discovered that he was still holding the hat in one hand and the ice-cream cone in the other. Luckily the cone was wrapped in paper. But as he ran he had squeezed the cone so that it had almost fallen apart in the middle. The warmth of his hand had begun to melt the ice cream.

It was the best kind, with hard chocolate on top. Absently he licked the chocolate off while he decided what to do.

He was standing outside a courtyard. A car drove in through the yard and disappeared out of sight under the building. There must be a garage down there.

Ben entered the courtyard hesitantly.

There he had an idea, a dangerous idea. The hat might help him if it was true that it could do magic. . . .

He crammed the hat on his head, feeling the same giddy sensation as the first time. It was the kind of feeling he had had in a dream once, when he was walking along the edge of a roof and was just about to throw himself into space in order to fly. . . .

A high-pitched, scornful laugh interrupted his thoughts.

✿ 21

A girl had come up from the garage and was standing beside the sign with PARKING FORBIDDEN written on it, laughing at him. He recognized her from school. She was in a grade ahead of him and her name was Barbie Reynolds.

"I've never seen anything more ridiculous than you," she said. "You look scared. Are you scared of something?"

"No, not at all," he said.

Then he said, "The police are after me."

Her eyes widened.

"For real?"

He nodded solemnly.

She took his hand and pulled him after her.

"Come on," she said. "I know where you can hide."

They ran down to the garage entrance and through the door, which was wide open. In there was an enormous space, larger than he could have dreamed. Cars were parked in neat rows in the parking bays, which were marked out in yellow paint on the concrete floor. One man had just parked his car and was getting out.

The children ran past him and squeezed between two cars that were standing close together. A man in oil-stained overalls was changing the engine oil in a car in the oil pit.

There was a strong smell of concrete, oil and gasoline. Ben liked it.

"Nobody can find us here," said Barbie.

They had crawled in behind a big stack of tires. It was like a little room in there. It smelled of rubber. Ben liked that too. He liked it when there was a strong smell of something: coffee, his mother's perfume, the spices in the cupboard, especially ginger, but not garlic. . . .

"What did you do?"

Ben did not answer at once. He had not yet recovered from his surprise. The hat had done its magic again!

A minute ago he had not known what to do and then he had put on the hat and Barbie had suddenly appeared as if from nowhere and helped him. He was safe here.

"Can't you watch out!"

The ice cream was dripping onto her dress. To make it up to her he handed over the cone. She stuck out her bottom lip but graciously accepted it. The ice cream was just one squashy mess by now.

She licked it, staring gravely at him all the while. Then she said:

"I like you very much already!"

He felt himself blushing. No one had said anything like that to him before. Except his mother, of course. But that was different.

He turned away and kicked the tires to cover his embarrassment.

"Don't look away," she said. "Do you know why I like you? Because you've got such big, serious eyes."

She must have sharp eyes herself to be able to see in this bad light. The roof was high and there were light bulbs hanging from it, but the light from each bulb didn't reach far. It was dark in all the corners. To him Barbie's face was a blur: a big mouth, a big nose and braids at the back.

He did not turn around again. He could hear her licking at his ice cream. Wasn't he going to get any more himself?

"Have you murdered someone?" she said.

Now he was forced to turn around.

"How could you think that?"

"Because the police are after you."

"There are other things," he said evasively.

"What, for instance?"

He had no answer to that. He hadn't really done anything.

Barbie ate the rest of the ice-cream cone and dropped the paper on the floor.

"Do you know why I don't like you?" she asked. "Because you're wearing that ridiculous hat. Why are you wearing that ridiculous hat?"

He took the hat off.

"Oh, no, put it on again! You look so funny when you've got it on."

Barbie was a strange girl. She made him nervous. Her voice sank to a whisper.

"Once I murdered a boy like you. Want to see?"

She took his hand again and pulled him behind her, farther into the little room. This time he pulled away. She nudged him.

"Put your hand in here and feel."

He did not move.

"Are you scared?"

He was.

"No," he said.

Hesitantly he put his hand between the tires. She pushed him impatiently. Gradually he felt farther and farther in. . . .

Suddenly his fingers met something cold and smooth. He shrieked.

Barbie laughed.

"You're scared now, aren't you?"

He leaned against the wall.

She put in her own hand and pulled out something that she held up in front of his face.

It was a plastic doll with no clothes on.

"How silly you are," she said.

He did not want to stay here with her. Just as he was making for the exit she stopped him with a tug at his sleeve.

"Can you hear?"

"What?"

"It sounds like a police car outside."

She put her face quite close to his and imitated the wail of a police siren in a low voice. Her breath was warm and smelled of chocolate.

"If you stay I'll look after you."

So he would be forced to stay. But he was beginning to feel hungry. This was the time he usually had milk and cookies at home.

Could it be true that the police were looking for him in a radio car? He listened hard. No, he could not hear anything. But you never knew. . . .

She put her arm around him.

"I'll look after you," she whispered.

One of her braids tickled his neck. He twisted away. He did not like people to come too close.

Through a gap between the tires he could see the man in overalls climbing out of the oil pit and going toward the exit. The man turned off the light in the garage and began to shut the doors.

Ben opened his mouth and drew in his breath to shout, but Barbie quickly put her hand over his mouth and whispered in his ear:

"Quiet! He may have gone for the police!"

The door was half closed now. Ben could see the sunlit section of the garage exit growing narrower and narrower and disappearing as the door slammed shut. It was pitch-black all around them.

✿ 22

They were locked in.

Ben was frightened. He could not understand why Barbie had not shouted to the man to wait for them. In the darkness the garage turned into a vast cave. He wanted to scream but he could not utter a sound. At the same time he was afraid to scream and reveal where he was.

Ghosts didn't exist and goblins didn't exist, except in fairy tales, but there were other things—nameless things.

He pushed his hand into his pocket and squeezed Woody. Feeling the smooth wood against his fingers calmed him down. Ever since he had been so small that he did not know how small he was, he had been afraid of the dark.

Barbie kept her arm around him. He did not pull away. It felt as if Barbie were his big sister. It would have been great fun to have a sister—or better still, a brother.

His eyes began to accustom themselves to the

darkness around them. It was not coal black, after all. A gray light filtered in through little windows with frosted glass on one side of the garage. That just made things worse. The light gleamed feebly on the car roofs. The cars looked like wet, kneeling elephants.

The nameless things were in the corners. They made no sound. They crept closer and closer on soft paws, until you felt a shaggy paw against your hand or a claw against your cheek. . . .

The terror was growing fast and he felt that he would not be able to bear it much longer.

"Are you scared?" whispered Barbie.

"Yes. Aren't you?"

"There's nothing dangerous here."

She had courage, he could tell that.

He remembered the doll—the murdered boy. The doll was over there in the corner. What if it belonged to the nameless ones . . . ?

He squeezed Woody hard and told himself again and again: There's no such thing as goblins, there's no such thing as goblins, there's no such thing as goblins. . . .

If anything could help him now it was the magic hat. With both hands he pulled it down on his head and waited.

"I have thought of something," whispered Barbie. "Hold my hand."

He gripped her hand. She was starting to squeeze out through the little space between the tires and the wall. Ben followed.

When they were out there was more light around them, but it was creepier, too. The garage was so big. There were no walls to shelter them.

The cars' headlights gleamed in the darkness where the light from the windows caught them. The cars seemed to be glaring at them with suspicious eyes, evil eyes.

Barbie's dress rustled.

The smell of oil filled his nose and the hat weighed on his head.

Barbie led him over to one of the cars and opened the door. The light immediately went on inside it. She pushed him into the front seat and sat behind the wheel herself. She slammed the door and the light went out.

"Are we allowed to do this?" Ben whispered.

"What they don't know won't hurt them," said Barbie easily. "Come closer."

He stayed where he was.

Barbie moved closer to him. She could not come very close because the gearshift was in the way.

Ben sighed. He felt safe in here, where he had walls around him.

The hat had done its magic again.

It was certainly not Woody who had helped him. Woody was a comfort, but he didn't do magic. But the hat did, Ben had to believe it now. He kept it on for safety's sake.

Two red eyes were looking at him about twenty yards away. One of the nameless ones? They did not move at all. They glowed red, like burning coal.

"Can you see the eyes?" he whispered.

She laughed.

"How silly you are! It's a machine that charges the batteries. When the light is on it tells you that the current is going through. Look."

From behind the steering wheel Barbie seemed to have no trouble finding the right knob and turning on the headlights. Two beams of light shot into the darkness and lit up the wall in front of them. There was a stack of car batteries and an apparatus with cables. In the middle of the apparatus were the two shining red eyes. Ben grinned.

Suddenly Barbie sounded the horn. Ben had never heard a more terrifying sound. It was as if the roof had fallen in. The sound echoed. Ben jumped.

"Do you know why I like you so much?" asked Barbie. "Because you're so scared. I can look after you."

Ben had no wish to be looked after, but just now it was good to have her with him, good that she was near.

In the silence that fell after the noise of the horn stopped he could hear her breathing. She was breathing through her nose. For some reason that made him hungry. Should he ask the hat for help?

Silently, inside himself, he said slowly and clearly, stressing every word: I would like something to eat.

Then he waited.

✤ 23

At first nothing happened. Barbie was sitting with both hands on the wheel, as if she were pretending to drive, and he was sitting beside her, his thoughts on the hat, and the headlights were shining on the wall and the red eyes were glowing by the batteries. Then she said:

"We can go now."

"But we are locked in," he said.

"You can open the door from inside."

She switched off the headlights and they got out. He went around to her side of the car and took her hand without being asked. The sound of their footsteps echoed softly against the walls. She asked him to wait inside the door while she stole out to make sure no one was waiting for them.

He stood with his back to the wall, trying to stop thinking about the nameless ones in the garage. They might get bolder now that he and Barbie were on their way out, they might make a last attempt to catch him. . . .

Barbie opened the door and slipped out. The sun was still shining outside and the light dazzled his eyes. He was surprised: He had thought that night had fallen long ago.

"The coast is clear!"

Ben hurried out. It was wonderful to escape from the darkness and feel the sun on his face again.

"I'm going to go home and eat now," said Barbie. "Coming?"

The magic had worked again, but now he was not in the least surprised.

"I want to go home," he said.

"Are you sure the police won't be waiting for you there?"

He was not sure, but he was a little scared of Barbie, she made him nervous. She did so many unexpected things.

"Coming?" she asked impatiently, putting out her hand.

He came, but refused to hold her hand. He didn't need that anymore.

Barbie lived on the first floor, just over the garage. She wanted him to leave his hat in the hall but Ben refused to part with it. He held on to it tightly when she tried to take it away from him.

Her parents were eating at the kitchen table. Her father was the man in overalls who had been in the garage, though he was not wearing overalls now. Now Ben knew why Barbie had felt so at home down there.

"Dad, this is Ben," said Barbie, "and he wants to eat with us. He can't go home because the police are waiting for him. He has murdered someone."

Ben was appalled, and disappointed too.

But her father did not seem worried. With a friendly smile he said:

"Don't you worry about Barbie, young man. She always talks too much. Do you like sausages?"

Ben nodded.

"There you are, then. You can sit on the sofa, opposite Barbie. If you sit beside her she'll never leave you in peace."

Barbie pouted and shook her head until the braids flew.

"Yes I will! I'm well behaved when I'm eating!"

It was not at all as Ben had imagined. Her father did not say a word about the police. Her mother fried some more sausages. He was allowed to keep his hat with him on the sofa.

Her father did not say much at all. He ate in huge mouthfuls, glancing from time to time at the newspaper, which he had open on the table.

Her mother had the same hair as Barbie, but knotted on the nape of her neck instead of braided.

She was wearing glasses. Ben stared at her until she said:

"Is there something wrong?"

"You're wearing glasses," said Ben.

"I don't see very well at short distances, you see."

"Neither do I," he said. "I have to wear glasses too. But they are at home now."

"Like to try mine?"

He put them on. Immediately, all the blurred contours around him cleared. He no longer had to strain to see things close to him, he could relax. It was good.

Barbie laughed.

"You look silly with glasses on."

"On the contrary," said her father. "People who wear glasses look smarter than anyone."

Ben smiled gratefully and stuck out his tongue at Barbie when no one was looking.

He liked being with this family.

⚘ 24

Barbie could not sit quiet and still for long. She tried to kick Ben's leg under the table, and she spilled milk on her father's paper.

And she told a frightful story about Ben.

"Ben," she said, "took the hat from a car parked in the street. At the same time—"

"I didn't!" said Ben.

"Quiet," said Barbie. "I know better than you. In any case, it's rude to interrupt."

Ben blushed.

"At the same time," Barbie went on, "Ben stole a blanket from the car, and a flashlight, and a doll. He tried to drive the car, but he couldn't do it. Then he saw a boy with an ice-cream cone and killed him and took the ice cream. He hid the boy in the garage. Now the police are after him and he can't go home, so wouldn't it be best if he stayed here tonight and I looked after him?"

Her parents did not agree with her and Ben was

glad. He enjoyed being here, but he did not want to stay for the night.

The extraordinary thing was that they listened to Barbie's story without minding a bit. When he told stories at home he always got into trouble. His father was very particular about telling the truth.

Barbie was allowed to finish her story without being interrupted. Then her father turned to Ben and asked:

"And what have you got to say?"

He had not been thinking of saying anything, but they looked at him in such a friendly way he decided to tell them the whole story, exactly as it had happened.

He left out a little: He did not dare tell a single soul that the hat was a magic hat—except Sammy. But Sammy was not here. He told them about the money and the woman and the ice cream and the newspaper stand he had knocked over, scattering papers all over the floor, and how he had run away and how he had met Barbie. He did not say anything about Woody, either. That was a secret.

Ben also told them his name and where he came from:

"My name is Ben Andrews and I live in the apartment by the park."

"Which park?" asked Mrs. Reynolds.

"Outside the school. On Ronaldsway."

"Does your dad have a telephone?"

"Yes." His dad's name was Keith Andrews and he was a mailman. His mother's name was Wendy and she taught at the high school.

Barbie's dad went out to the hall, telephoned and came back to say that Ben's mother had been worried about him. There were no policemen waiting for him at home, and no shopkeeper, either.

Ben breathed a deep sigh of relief. He gave back the glasses and thanked Barbie's mother for the meal. Barbie went home with him, because she knew the way.

It was not as far as he had thought. They were soon back at home on Ronaldsway. He said goodbye to her as soon as he saw his house, but Barbie insisted on accompanying him all the way home.

She even went inside and rode up in the elevator with him.

"I've never been in an elevator before," she said.

She no longer looked quite so sure of herself and that pleased Ben. At last there was something he knew better than she did.

Barbie was being quiet, for a change. She liked going so far up in the elevator.

Ben kicked the wall a bit as he used to do with Sammy, but now that Sammy was not there it was not the same. It was not at all the same. Barbie did not know what it meant.

She did not get out when the elevator stopped. She just said good-bye and Ben showed her which button to press to go down. She pressed the button and disappeared, and he rang at the door marked "Andrews."

✤ 25

His father and mother were both at home. That was unusual. Dad was often at meetings in the evening and Mom worked on committees.

"Where have you been?" asked his mother.

He told them about Barbie and her parents and the garage and the woman. But he said nothing about the hat being magical.

Mom was not angry with him. She was seldom angry, in fact, she was understanding. It was too bad that in the daytime she was at school. Of course he was at school too, but he came home much earlier.

It made life lonely, especially now that Sammy was gone.

Dad was not interested in where he had been, but he did want to know how he had got the hat. When Ben said that a man on the park bench had thrown the hat away and he had picked it up, a dissatisfied frown appeared on Dad's forehead.

"How do you know he was throwing it away?"

"He said so," said Ben.

"He may have regretted it later," said Dad. "He may have come back to look for it. You'll have to go back to the park tomorrow and put it on the bench."

Ben's stomach turned cold, as if he had been eating too much ice cream. That was impossible. He could not do without his hat.

"It's my hat!" he said desperately.

Dad looked at him with his stern look.

"There's no more to be said," he said. "You will take the hat back tomorrow."

Ben knew that it was useless to protest when Dad's mind was made up. He could be very strict.

⚜ 26

Ben went to his room to do some homework but he found it difficult to concentrate. He could think of nothing but the hat. He had not even been allowed to take it to his room. It was hanging on the hat rack out in the hall.

The sun had gone down and it was twilight.

Ben's eyes were tired. His eyes were often tired in the evening, and having his glasses on didn't make any difference.

It was time to go to bed. He took a book with him, not a school book, but a nice book he had borrowed from the library. It was called *Dr. Dolittle's Post Office* and it was about a doctor who understood the speech of animals and could talk to them.

Mom had forbidden him to read in bed because his eyes got so tired, but he could not do without reading something every night.

When there was a knock on the door he quickly hid the book under the covers. It was really a game, because Mom and Dad knew that he read for a little while before they came in to say good night. But they said nothing. Only if he was very tired the next morning, Mom might remind him that he was not allowed to read in bed.

Mom and Dad came to say good night to him every night. He knew that even if Dad came home late and he had been in bed for a long time, Dad would look in and whisper good night although Ben was asleep and could not hear him.

Dad usually put just his head in, but Mom always came over to the bed, smoothed the sheet and plumped up the pillows and talked to him for a while. When he was smaller, she used to read him a story. He wanted her to do that now, too, but she did not have time.

Before she went out she turned off the ceiling light. He was allowed to turn off the reading lamp beside the bed for himself. As soon as she had shut the door he took out the book from under the blankets, put it on the chair beside the bed, and turned off the light. Then he pulled the blankets right up to his chin, curled up and tried to sleep.

He could not stop thinking about the hat. It seemed to him like a living creature, and now it was hanging, lonely and deserted, on the hat rack in the hall.

He could not sleep, however hard he tried. That

was not only because of the hat but also because of Sammy. Mostly because of Sammy.

The worst thing was that he could not share the secret of the hat with Sammy. They had always shared all their secrets.

It was not nearly as much fun to have a secret on your own. Sammy might even have thought of a way of keeping the hat. He was so full of ideas. What if Sammy were to come back tomorrow?

That was a good thought. It made him feel calm and sleepy.

Before he slid down into sleep he thought a little bit about Barbie. She wanted to "look after him." He could look after himself!

Soon he fell asleep.

❧ 27

He did not seem to have been asleep long when he woke up again. It was the middle of the night.

He had been dreaming that he and Sammy were playing together and Sammy came back with him and they were together in his room.

Ben looked around him. The room was not quite dark. A feeble, cold moonlight shone in through the window. Everything that was gray or white seemed to have become luminous: an open arithmetic book on the table, the pale wallpaper, the picture with the seven gnomes dancing in a meadow, a china dog.

Sammy was not there.

Ben returned slowly from his dream. Sammy had been just as close to him as Barbie had been in the garage that day. He had been able to hear him breathing. Could you hear sounds in dreams?

He was disturbed, but not for Sammy's sake. It was something else, but he did not know what.

He tried to go back to sleep, but only succeeded

in waking up more and more. He tossed and turned in the bed. The moonlight made the room cold, but it was so hot under the blankets that he felt sticky. He had to throw off the covers. Suddenly he knew what it was that was disturbing him.

The hat.

The magic hat was out in the hall, lonely and forgotten. He didn't like it. All at once it was absolutely necessary for him to get it.

For a few seconds he lay listening to hear if his mother and father were awake but he could not hear a sound.

He climbed out of bed and tiptoed on bare feet to the window, across the chilly linoleum floor. He had to have a look at the moonlight first.

He was surprised to see how light the sky was. The moon was full, almost round, like a wheel. He felt an extraordinary excitement. It was as if the moon had spoken to him:

"Up so late, all by yourself? Aren't you frightened?"

Well, yes, he was a little frightened.

He dug in the pocket of his pants, which were hanging over the back of a chair, and took out Woody. It was comforting to hold Woody in his hand.

He tiptoed across the floor and opened the door

cautiously. It squeaked a little. He had never noticed that before, but at night it was so quiet that you could hear the slightest sound.

He held his breath for a few seconds but nothing happened. The living room was in darkness but he knew exactly where the furniture was. With outstretched hands, he crossed the room and reached the hall without mishap.

He wondered if he dared turn on the light. It would be safest not to. He knew where the hat was, at the other end, on the hat rack.

He could not reach it.

He went into the kitchen to get a chair.

The kitchen lay in half darkness. The moonlight was shining on the taps and the stove and the metal corners on the cupboard and the knives hanging up on the magnetic board over the counter.

Were the nameless things here, at home, too?

That was a stupid thought. He regretted having thought it, but it was too late. The darkness thickened in every nook and cranny. Absolutely anything might be hiding there.

Ben longed to be back in bed, safe in his own room.

In the deep silence he heard the sound of the elevator on its way up. He held his breath and listened. The elevator sang its way past their apartment and continued upward. It stopped. A few seconds later it came down again and then there was silence, even more than before.

With endless care he carried the kitchen chair out into the hall. He climbed onto the chair and was seized with dizziness. There was no point for him to fix his eyes on and it made him sway to and fro, like a tree in a storm. He succeeded in catching hold of the hat rack. Then he stretched out his hand, found the hat and put it on his head.

He got down from the chair and carried it back to the kitchen.

When he came out to the hall again he did not walk across the middle of the room; instead he kept close to the walls. That was a mistake. He had forgotten that Dad's umbrella was leaning against the wall.

The umbrella fell to the floor and Ben jumped. Panic-stricken, he picked up the umbrella and stood rigidly waiting for the catastrophe to happen.

The door to Mom and Dad's bedroom opened and Mom came out. She switched on the light in the living room.

Ben managed to send a thought up to the hat: "Help me now. Don't let Mom be angry."

And his mother was not angry. She smiled, not a happy smile but a smile of relief at finding him unhurt.

No, she was not angry. She went up to him, leaned over him and stretched out her arms.

"My dear, what is the matter?" she said.

Ben threw himself into her arms, hat, umbrella and all and hugged her hard and was hugged back just as hard.

It was not very often that he did that kind of thing, but it felt wonderful.

He was safe now, the darkness had been chased away, the nameless things did not exist, everything was all right.

A little later he explained to his mother why he had felt it was necessary to get up. His mother gave him a glass of milk and a slice of cake and he went back to bed and fell asleep at once. The hat was with him. It sat on the chair beside his bed and it was not lonely and forgotten anymore.

❦ 28

It was raining and there was the smell of tobacco when Ben woke up.

It was the first time there had been the smell of tobacco in Ben's room. Dad didn't smoke. Mom smoked cigarettes but she never smoked in there.

Then he saw the hat on the chair beside the bed, the green-brown speckly magic hat from Scotland. He smiled. It was like seeing a dear old friend again.

Instead of lying in bed enjoying himself, as he usually did, he got up and dressed quickly.

He decided to do one more bit of magic before giving the hat back. Perhaps the hat itself would help him so that they would not have to be parted.

He tugged the cord for Sammy. There was no answer. He had tugged the cord several times a day during the last few days but he had never had an answer.

Dead—what did it mean? You were gone, but what else?

He had hot chocolate for breakfast as usual.

Mom had made the chocolate from the box with *Bournville Cocoa* written on it. She always put twice the right amount of powder in the cup so he could eat a little before she added the hot milk. He loved eating the powder. He scraped his spoon on the bottom of the cup and made a white cross of sugar in the brown stuff.

The cold powder tasted good. He licked his spoon slowly.

Then Mom poured in the hot milk and the chocolate powder dissolved in the milk and the milk grew browner and browner.

Dad was in the bathroom, shaving. Sometimes he tried to sing. It sounded horrible. He was not singing today; perhaps the bad weather depressed him.

When he went off to school his father said:

"You won't forget to return the hat this afternoon, will you?"

Ben promised.

He could not take the hat to school with him and perhaps that was a good thing because he would not have been able to concentrate at all during the lessons. It was bad enough as it was.

The teacher gave him an anxious look.

"Don't sit there dreaming, Ben."

Her voice was kind, actually a little bit unhappy, but there was nothing to be unhappy about, was there?

Perhaps she was unhappy because it was raining.

He himself was not unhappy about the rain. If he was unhappy, it was because of the hat. Then he began to think about Sammy.

He kept his thoughts about Sammy deep inside himself. He didn't talk about Sammy. *Sammy* was a forbidden word.

Every morning Ben hoped Sammy would come and ring the doorbell as he used to, but he never did. Every morning he hoped that Sammy would be down in the courtyard waiting so they could go to school together, but he was never there. Every morning he hoped that they would meet at school, but Sammy never came.

It was raining, but there was no wind.

During recess he caught a glimpse of Barbie. Once they bumped into each other outside the door and they were as close together as they had been in her house, but Barbie pretended not to have seen him. It was as if they had never met. Ben said nothing, either.

It rained all day.

Finally the time came when he had to return the hat. The hat was to do its magic for the last time. It was very sad.

For safety's sake he went the same way as before. It was raining hard and he was wearing his rain clothes. None of the other children were out.

At last he reached the park and was peering through the hedge. The park was deserted, the bench empty.

Slowly he approached the bench. It was wet and did not look inviting.

It did not seem possible that the man and the woman would come back in this weather. As far as he could see there was only one thing to do: Put the hat on the bench, go home again and forget all about it.

Ben knew that he had to return the hat. It would be no good going home and telling his father that he hadn't gotten rid of the hat just because it was raining. No excuses would do for Dad, he knew that.

But he had one spell left. Slowly and ceremoniously he took the hat in both hands, raised it up and put it on his head.

A shiver of expectation ran through him.

He had an idea and it seemed to be a good one. He would let the hat itself decide its fate. Ben smiled happily.

Carefully he put the hat down on the bench, retreated and hid behind the nearest maple tree. Then he waited.

✤ 29

It was a long wait. The wind rose after a time, the rain increased and began to tear off the yellow leaves of the maple tree. They fell all around him.

One of the leaves sailed down and landed on the middle of the crown of the hat.

Nothing happened for a long time. The park was, and remained, empty. The schoolyard on the other side of the road was deserted and lifeless. The windows were dark.

The rain slackened as the wind tore holes in the clouds. An ice-cold raindrop fell on Ben's neck and rolled down his back. He shivered and shook himself.

Kevin came by with one of the small boys, called Ian. Both of them lived in his building.

They went into the park, kicking the leaves and looking around them in the way people do when they have nothing to do and hope that something will happen.

Kevin didn't see Ben, but he suddenly caught sight of the hat.

"Look!" he said.

He and Ian ran to the bench and picked up the hat. Ben wanted to shout but he kept quiet. Who could tell—that might be part of the hat's magic.

Kevin put the hat on his head and Ben's fists knotted with bitterness. Then Ian tried on the hat, which came down over his ears. Kevin laughed aloud. Ian pulled the hat off his head in a huff and threw it on the grass.

Ben could not help feeling a little glad in spite of all his worry. It was obvious that the hat would do no magic for Kevin and Ian. Only for him, Ben.

He had hoped that they would leave the hat to its fate and go on their way, but he was not as lucky as all that.

First Kevin kicked the hat a few times, and it hurt Ben to watch; then Kevin put the hat on his head and walked away.

Ben thought furiously. What was he to do? What would Sammy have done?

Ben knew: Sammy was brave, he would have protected the hat. Ben stepped out from behind the tree and shouted:

"Kevin! That's my hat!"

Kevin turned around.

"What did you say?"

"That's my hat," said Ben. "Give it to me!"

Kevin shook his head.

"It's not your hat. I found it here on the bench."

"I just put it there," said Ben. "It belongs to a man."

"What man?" asked Kevin.

"Just a man," said Ben lamely.

Kevin shrugged his shoulders.

"You're nuts!"

He pulled the hat further over his forehead and went on walking.

Ben did not want to fight Kevin, who was twice as strong as he was and two years older.

Actually, Kevin was right: It was not Ben's hat.

Ben watched helplessly as Kevin and Ian walked away. Before they disappeared behind the hedge Kevin took off the hat and waved it in the air, as if in triumph. There were tears in Ben's eyes.

The hat had disappointed him. It had not done any magic. Or still worse; maybe it had done its magic in reverse, in order to leave him.

Heavy-footed, he began to walk back through the park.

As he reached the pavement he bumped into a

man and woman on their way into the park. He could not believe his eyes. It was the man who owned the hat.

He was wearing another hat today, a much smarter one, less crumpled. He was walking arm in arm with the woman and they were looking happy in the rain.

"Hello!" said Ben breathlessly. "Can I have your hat?"

The man looked surprised.

"You want my hat? What for?"

"I don't mean that hat," said Ben. "I mean the hat you threw away."

"How did you know about that?"

"I was behind the tree, watching," said Ben.

The woman laughed.

"Do you mean yesterday?"

"Yes," said Ben shyly.

Both of them laughed, as if it had been a great joke.

"What happened then?" she said.

"I took the hat with me," said Ben. "But when I came home Dad said I couldn't keep it. He said I was to give it back to the owner."

"So you have been waiting here for me?" he asked.

"Yes," said Ben. "But Kevin and Ian came and took the hat and went off with it."

"No damage done," said the man. "As you can see, I have bought a new hat. And if you should come across the hat again, it's yours. I solemnly resign all rights in the hat to you!"

Ben flushed with happiness.

"Thanks very much!"

Now all he had to do was to get the hat back again.

❧ 30

Ben crossed the road slowly, deep in thought.

For the hundredth time he wished that Sammy were with him. It was much easier to think when there were two of you. Everything was easier when there were two of you.

It was unthinkable that he should fight Kevin for the hat. It was even more unthinkable that the hat would be returned to him voluntarily. He would have to be smart.

Wandering along as he was, thinking and not looking where he was going, he found himself in front of Barbie's house. Her father was standing in front of it, filling a car tank from a gasoline can.

"Hello," said Ben.

"Hello," said her father. "If you're looking for Barbie, she's down in the garage, chasing a bird. Or was it me you wanted?"

Ben shook his head. Actually he had not meant to come here at all, but when he thought about it, it did not seem such a silly idea after all. Barbie might be able to help him think. She was full of ideas.

"I have come to see Barbie," he said.

He went down to the garage. Barbie's father had said something about her chasing a bird. What could that mean?

He soon found out.

There were not many cars inside. Barbie was running about, clapping her hands. When she caught sight of him she called:

"Come here and help me!"

"What are you doing?"

"I'm trying to chase out a bird," said Barbie. "It flew in here to get out of the rain but then it got frightened and now it keeps flying straight into the window, trying to get out. I am afraid it will hurt itself."

Just then there was a rushing sound above Ben's head and he saw the bird flying straight into one of the frosted windows. It thumped against the glass, flapped wildly and fell softly to the floor, out of sight behind a car. Barbie ran toward it.

Ben was the first to see the bird, which was lying in a corner, not moving. Cautiously they went closer.

The bird was lying still with its wings outspread and its beak on the concrete floor.

"It's not moving," said Ben.

"It's probably dead," said Barbie.

She nudged it with the toe of her shoe.

The eye seemed to be covered with a gray film. The head was dusty.

"It's dead," said Barbie.

At that moment they heard the same kind of thumping against the window as before. They looked up. There was another bird.

"Come on," said Barbie. "We've got to chase it out before it hurts itself."

They left the motionless bird and ran after the other, which was tumbling about near the window. They got behind it, clapped their hands and shooed it away. Terrified, the bird fluttered toward the doors, the children behind it.

The bird swerved to and fro for a time and then, all of a sudden, it was out in the open, flying away.

Barbie gave a deep sigh of relief and pleasure.

"It must be glad now that we helped it out," she said.

"Yes," said Ben.

He felt proud too. It was nice to have done something good.

"Now we must bury the dead bird," said Barbie.

They went back to the dead bird in the corner. Ben looked wonderingly at it. It was dead, but it had not gone yet. It was here, he could touch it if he wanted to. And yet in a certain way it had gone.

There was a film over its eyes, it was blind, motionless and dusty.

Ben nudged it with his boot. It was nothing to be afraid of, and nothing to be unhappy about, either.

The bird was dead. Sammy was dead too. Suddenly Sammy had moved away, out of reach. In that moment Ben understood something important: Even if Sammy had been there, so close that Ben could touch him, it would have been meaningless. He knew now that Sammy would never come back again.

"Why are you looking so unhappy?" asked Barbie. "The other bird got away all right!"

"I was just thinking about something," he muttered.

He was a little bit unhappy, deep inside.

"I know what we'll do," said Barbie eagerly. "We'll bury the bird and we'll have a priest to make a speech and everything. I've got a cardboard box we can put the bird in."

Ben began to feel happier. Yes, that was the right thing to do. The bird must not be left to lie here alone, getting dustier and dustier. A car might run over it. It must be buried in a safe place where it would be in peace.

Barbie ran for the cardboard box and they moved the bird into it. The bird was very light.

They laid it out beautifully, with its wings folded, as they should be, and closed the lid.

"But where shall we bury the box?" said Barbie. "There's no earth here."

"There's the park," said Ben.

They went back to the block where Ben lived, Barbie carrying the box with the bird in it.

✾ 31

It was raining hard.

They would need a spade. Ben knew where he could get one. He went over to the babies' sandbox near his apartment house and, sure enough, there was a toy spade in the sand.

He picked it up and was just going to run back to Barbie when he heard a cross voice behind him:

"That's my spade! Leave it alone!"

Ian and Kevin and Ollie were standing in the doorway, out of the rain. Kevin was holding the hat. It was Ian who had shouted.

"I only want to borrow it," said Ben.

"You're not allowed," said Ian.

Ben had an idea.

"We want it for a funeral," he said. "You can come too, if I can borrow the spade."

"Who are you going to bury?" asked Kevin.

"A bird," said Ben.

Barbie was not pleased when Ben came back with a whole gang, but she brightened up when she caught sight of the hat in Kevin's hand.

"The priest can wear that as a priest's hat," she said.

"Then I've got to be the priest," said Kevin.

"Ben's got to be the priest, because it's his hat," said Barbie firmly.

"I'm the biggest," said Kevin.

"Then you can be the mourner and make the speech," said Barbie.

"What about me?" asked Ian.

"You can dig the grave," said Barbie.

She opened the lid and let everyone admire the bird. Then they crawled through the hole in the hedge and went into the park. They found a good place where Ian started to dig.

The rain stopped and the sun came out from behind a cloud.

When the hole was deep enough Barbie ordered Kevin to hand over the hat to Ben. Kevin was unwilling, but in the end he gave in. He said:

"What does a mourner do?"

"Make a speech," said Barbie. "You've got to say how good this bird was when it was alive, and all that."

"What does a priest do?" asked Ben.

"He takes his hat off when we put the box in the hole," said Barbie. "And then he throws in a little earth. Then he reads something from the Bible. Do you know anything from the Bible?"

"Sure thing," said Ben.

He put on the hat and just as he did so he had the same quivery feeling as before. The magic power had not gone out of it, he was certain of that.

They stood side by side. It was a solemn moment.

"Now," said Barbie.

She took the box and placed it in the hole. Ben removed his hat and shoveled a little earth in with the spade. The earth fell on the lid of the box with a dull sound.

Without really knowing why, he said one word inside himself:

"Sammy."

What he was doing was important. It was as if he were saying good-bye to Sammy, although it was a bird they were burying.

Barbie nudged him and said impatiently:

"Come on then, say it!"

In a sing-song voice Ben said:

"Gentle Jesus meek and mild, look upon a little child. Pity my simplicity, suffer me to come to Thee. . . ."

Ian and Ollie stood by, open-mouthed, silent and impressed.

Kevin cleared his throat in embarrassment.

"Now you say something!" whispered Barbie.

"I don't know what to say."

"Something about the bird being good."

"Dear bird . . ." said Kevin, and then came to a stop.

He stood in silence for some time, wriggling. Then it came:

"You were a good bird while you were alive and you flew very well and we are glad you're dead and all right and can go to heaven."

Kevin stopped, out of breath.

There was a few seconds' silence. Then Ian whispered cautiously:

"Is it over now?"

"Yes," said Barbie shortly. "Fill the grave in again."

Ian picked up his spade and shoveled the earth back into the hole. Ollie helped him with a bit of wood.

Ben put on his hat and expressed a passionate wish inside himself:

"I want to keep my magic hat!"

Ben glanced at Kevin and realized that wishing would not be enough. Kevin had no intention of returning the hat.

Barbie broke off a rose that was growing nearby and laid it on the mound of earth. Then the funeral was over.

❦ 32

The man who looked as if he didn't like children came out onto the porch. The children ran away as fast as they could, running behind the toolshed, climbing the fence, pushing their way through the hedge and bursting into the park.

"Give me the hat!" said Kevin.

Ben was wearing the hat, but he was no longer a priest.

"It's my hat," said Ben.

"Prove it," said Kevin.

Ben couldn't do that. The man who owned the hat and the woman had gone away. The park was empty.

"You've got no right . . ." Ben began.

"Give me the hat," said Kevin. "I'm stronger than you."

Ben knew Kevin was stronger than he was and could run faster than he could.

Suddenly Kevin laughed.

"I have an idea," he said. "I could take the hat

off you as easy as anything if I wanted, but I've thought of something better. We'll have a contest for it. The winner gets the hat."

"What sort of contest?" asked Ben.

"A race," said Ian brightly.

"Or a long jump," said Ollie.

"There's no fun in that," said Kevin in a superior voice. "Ben wouldn't have a chance."

"Have a contest to see who's the bravest," said Barbie.

Kevin brightened.

"I know!" he said, pulling a fairly clean handkerchief out of his pocket. "I'll climb that tree and tie my handkerchief as high as I can. If you can bring it down again, Ben, you can keep the hat. Do you agree?"

Ben frowned. He was not particularly good at climbing. If you were going to climb trees it was better to be able to see clearly. His glasses were at home.

Ben looked at Barbie and Barbie looked back. She looked straight into his eyes, as if she were trying to encourage him. Or perhaps she was expecting something of him? Ben nodded.

"Okay," said Kevin. "But remember, you are doing it at your own risk."

He sought out the biggest maple in the park and they all gathered underneath it.

The first problem was how Kevin could get to the lowest branches. They were much too high and the trunk was much too thick for him to shinny up.

In the end Ben had to stand underneath the tree while Barbie helped Kevin onto Ben's shoulders. Then Kevin caught hold of the lowest branch and swung himself up.

He sat still for a moment, puffing.

"That was hard," he said. "Stay underneath in case I fall."

He began the climb. It was quite easy to begin with. The branches were close together. He worked his way upward rapidly, but as he drew nearer to the top of the tree it began to shake and sway and yellow leaves floated down.

After a while Kevin called:

"I'll soon be as high as those clouds!"

But he was exaggerating.

Later still:

"I can't get any higher now."

The tree shook and a lot of leaves fell. After another minute or two he came scrambling down. He hung from the lowest branch, dropped and landed on the ground with a thud. He looked at Ben.

"Now it's your turn."

✿ 33

Ben went up to the tree, still wearing the hat.
"Take the hat off," said Kevin.

Ben refused. This was the worst thing he had
ever let himself in for and if he was to have a
chance of success he needed all the help he could
get—from the magic hat and from Woody.

Kevin shrugged his shoulders.

"Suit yourself. You look ridiculous, climbing a
tree with a hat on."

Ben did not care whether he looked ridiculous
or not. Barbie helped him onto Kevin's shoulders
and he took a firm grip of the lowest branch and
swung himself up. It was very hard work in his
heavy boots, but Kevin had been wearing boots
too. He kept still for a moment, getting his breath
back, just as Kevin had done before beginning the
climb.

It went easily to start with, almost like climbing
a ladder. But after a while he came to a hard part.
He had to put his foot on a rotten branch while he

reached for a handhold higher up. He had difficulty calculating the distance to the branch he was supposed to be holding. He could not see it clearly and the more he strained to see it the more blurred it became, because there were tears in his eyes.

"How's it going?" Barbie called from the ground.

Ben did not answer. He had to concentrate. He put his hand in his pocket and squeezed Woody. Then he clenched his teeth, put his foot on the rotten branch and heaved himself up.

He had been prepared for the branch to crack. At the very moment the rotten branch gave way with a loud snap he grasped the higher branch with his hands. For a few seconds he hung there, clinging tightly to the trunk with feet and knees. His arms hurt.

He slowly worked his way upward, finding a hold on an even higher branch, and succeeded in getting his leg over a thick branch, where he sat for a long time getting his breath back. His heart was hammering in his chest.

He felt quite proud. He had made it.

But he was tired. One of his boots seemed to be sliding off. That gave him an idea.

"Look out down there!" he shouted.

Then he shook off both boots and let them fall. It was easier to climb now. He could get a better grip with his feet. His boots had been slipping on the rain-soaked branches. He looked up and saw the handkerchief, which was stuck in a fork high above him. It was so high that he could scarcely believe it.

He went on, very slowly and carefully. It had been very silly of him to get involved in this contest just for the sake of an old hat. Or was that the only reason? He wouldn't have done it if Barbie had not been there. He wouldn't have done it if he had not had the hat on him, either. If it really was a magic hat, it should be able to help him now.

What would Sammy have done in his place? Sammy was brave, but that didn't matter anymore. Sammy was not there. Sammy was gone forever. Ben was alone now, alone with the hat.

Suddenly both feet skidded and he was hanging by his arms. The jerk was so violent that he thought his arms would give way. It hurt terribly. But his hands, gripping the branches above his head, did not give way. They hung on.

He made a great effort, got back onto the branch and climbed on.

The near-accident had scared him, but at the same time it made him braver and stronger. He was firmly intent on bringing back that handkerchief, which was beckoning him on so teasingly.

He was not far from it now.

112

The tree swayed beneath him. What if it should give way! But of course it had held Kevin, and Kevin was heavier than he was.

He looked down. He should not have done that: He felt dizzy. He was forced to hang on tightly to the trunk, hugging it and closing his eyes. There he sat, with his eyes shut, his heart pumping violently, for a long time, until the feeling of panic passed. He made up his mind not to look down again.

Now the handkerchief was only a yard above him, but it seemed impossible to climb anymore. The branches were thin and weak near the top.

He wished he had a stick with him, with which to poke the handkerchief down. Then he stopped wishing he had a stick with him. It would have been cheating. He had a feeling that the hat did not like cheating, and neither did Barbie.

The tree swayed. He did not dare to climb any higher. It was annoying to have to give up so close to the goal, but only a nut would go on, only a dummy would climb any further. It was pointless to act dumb. Mom and Dad would not want him to take a risk like that. It was no trouble for Kevin, who could see well and was nimbler and stronger, too.

But Ben knew that it was no good thinking up a lot of excuses. He had decided, once and for all, to get that handkerchief down, no matter what happened. It was very important. He did not know quite how he would do it, he just knew he had to. He knew it deep inside himself. It was important.

Now he could not even touch Woody anymore because he had to hold on with both hands. The worst thing was that the hat was in the way. It had twisted around on his head and seemed to be weighing him down on one side.

He was very high now. He looked down again, he couldn't help it. But it was not so bad this time. He was so high that it was almost like looking down from his own window in the apartment. If you were up high enough you didn't get dizzy.

He had once flown in a plane with Dad and Mom. It had not bothered him at all, he had not been the least bit afraid. And yet they had been so high then that the boats down in the water below had been as small as the head of a matchstick.

He looked out over the surrounding country. He could see a long, long way; the cars driving along the road, the traffic circle, the block of apartments. He could almost imagine that he could make out the chocolate box in the kitchen window at home, the one with *Bournville Cocoa* on it. But of course that was impossible.

To his surprise Ben discovered that he was enjoying being high up in the air. At that moment, sitting near the top of the high maple tree, he dreamed once again of being able to fly.

"Are you stuck?" shouted Barbie from the ground below. "Are you scared?"

Ben smiled to himself. No, he wasn't scared anymore.

He felt an entirely new, wonderful certainty as he approached the final stage. He climbed slowly and extremely carefully, a few inches at a time. Then he stretched up and felt about with his fingers, his face so close to the trunk that he could smell the scent of the rain-soaked bark. He touched the handkerchief.

It was not tied on, just jammed into a fork. He tugged at it and it was in his hand.

But he was not satisfied. Stuffing the handkerchief in his pocket, he took out Woody. For the last time he looked at Woody and whispered to himself:

"Bye now, Woody."

Then he pushed Woody into the fork as hard as he could and began to climb down.

The downward climb took a long time, but he said nothing until he had jumped to the ground and the others were looking at him, eager and expectant.

"Give me the hat," said Kevin.

"Why?" said Ben.

"You haven't got the handkerchief, have you?" asked Kevin.

Ben pulled the handkerchief out of his pocket and threw it to Kevin.

"Here it is," he said.

Kevin looked disappointed, but Barbie and Ian and Ollie gazed admiringly at Ben. He said nothing about leaving Woody up there. He would never tell anyone that. Woody had been his and Sammy's secret. Now he was not needed anymore. He would be stuck in the fork at the top of the maple tree for all eternity.

✿ 34

Then something extraordinary happened: Ben suggested that they should go home and play ball in the yard. It was the first time that Ben had made a suggestion and the strangest thing of all was that his friends agreed.

"Okay," said Kevin. "Let's go!"

And off they ran.

Ben came last because he had to put on his boots first, but that did not matter. In some way, he was first at that particular moment, whatever happened. He felt it and it looked as if the others felt it. Tomorrow everything would probably be the same as before, and he would be the one who was not allowed to join in and play because he was so clumsy and saw so badly, but it was a long time till tomorrow. And he had a vague suspicion that the situation had changed. His friends no longer regarded him as a dunce. He had succeeded in beating Kevin.

He ran after the others, stumbled and fell.

"Damn!" he said.

He got up and went on.

They played ball in the yard for some time. Barbie joined in too. Ben kept his hat on but no one laughed at him or thought he looked ridiculous.

When it was time to go in for supper, Barbie came with him. He had asked her if she would like to come up with him and she had said yes at once.

Inside the elevator she looked at him in the mirror and said:

"You look dumb in that hat."

"It's a magic hat," he said.

Just as he had said it he remembered it was a secret. He had never meant to talk about it to anyone. It was to have been a secret as Woody had been a secret between him and Sammy.

"Really and truly?" asked Barbie.

She was not laughing at him.

He nodded.

"It's already done magic for me several times," he said. "Would you like to try it on?"

Barbie took the hat and put it on her head. It came right down to her eyebrows. Her braids stuck out behind. She looked very funny and Ben laughed.

She made a face at him in the mirror.

"You're the one who looks dumb now," he said.

The elevator stopped at the fifth floor. They got out and Ben asked:

"Did you wish something?"

Barbie nodded vigorously.

"What?" asked Ben.

Barbie shook her head.

"I'm not going to tell."

Ben was pleased. You should never give away a wish. That meant it wouldn't work.

Ben rang the bell and his mom opened the door. She looked at Barbie in surprise.

"This is Barbie," said Ben. "Can she have supper with us?"

Barbie said, "Hello." Ben's mom then turned to him disapprovingly.

"I thought Dad said you were to give the hat back this afternoon."

"I met the man who owned the hat," said Ben. "He had bought a new one. He gave me this one."

The wrinkles disappeared from his mother's forehead.

"Well, that should be all right then, I suppose," she said.

They had sausages and omelettes for supper.

Ben's dad was at a meeting.

After supper Ben and Barbie went to Ben's

room and as soon as they were inside the door Barbie whispered excitedly:

"Do you know what I wished in the elevator?"

"No!" said Ben.

"That we should have sausages for supper!"

Ben felt a little shy with Barbie when he was alone with her in his room. No one but Sammy had played with him there before.

Barbie went around looking at everything, at the little china dog Ben called Max and at his books and at the picture of the seven gnomes dancing in the meadow and at the clay mask his uncle had brought home from Africa.

She also went over to the window and looked out.

"What's this?" she said, pointing to the cord that was hanging out through the ventilator.

"Nothing special," said Ben.

He opened the window, pulled the cord out through the ventilator and dropped it.

He shut the window and sat down on the bed. Barbie sat down by the table and began to play with the china dog. It was strange to be alone with Barbie, not because she was a girl; but because she was strange.

But that wasn't quite right either. She was not completely strange and she was getting less and less strange every minute. Suddenly Ben thought to himself: Tomorrow I can go and meet Barbie. We can be together and play.

That was a good thought.

Barbie looked up from Max, the china dog, and asked:

"Why did you drop the cord that was hanging by the window?"

Ben hesitated for a few seconds and then he told her about Sammy and the cord. He talked for a long time and Barbie listened in silence. He liked her for not interrupting him.

Then they played Scrabble. And then Ben got out his water colors and they painted for a long time. They discovered that they both loved painting. They played together so long that his mother had to knock on the door to tell them that it was late and time for Barbie to go home.

Ben took her home, wearing his hat.

When they parted outside her door he gave her the biggest present he could think of. He said:

"Would you like to keep the hat till tomorrow?"

She looked serious.

"Why do you want me to?"

"Because I like you," Ben said quickly and shyly.

She put on the hat and smiled.

"I like you very much, too," she said. "Do you know why? Because you are good."

Ben turned and ran home, bareheaded. It was late but he wasn't tired. Actually he felt wonderful. He would be seeing Barbie and the hat again tomorrow. Anything in the world might happen.